1 It came from Outer Space

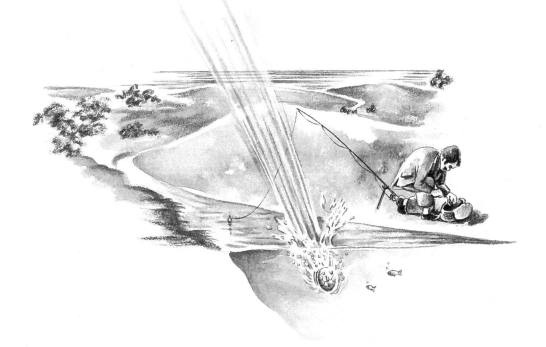

A hundred years ago Southbeach was one of the prettiest places in England. Green fields, clean beaches, sparkling streams. It was the last place on earth that an ordinary fisherman would have expected to see a visitor from Outer Space. And thank goodness he didn't! But it was there all the same. Some sort of probe from hundreds of light years away. It landed in a stream near Southbeach and settled there quietly for the next century.

Those hundred years brought a lot of changes to Southbeach. Traffic, buildings, pollution . . . So it was a very different stream that the two friends Jenny and Amina were walking beside one day in early summer.

"It's disgusting!" said Amina. She felt very strongly about things like people throwing their rubbish into rivers. She felt strongly about Martin Rowlands too. She wouldn't go so far as to call him disgusting but he was certainly no friend of hers and now he suddenly turned up, spoiling her walk with Jenny.

Jenny went up to Martin who seemed to be feeling ill, but he was as unfriendly as ever.

"I don't need your help," he snapped. But Jenny wouldn't give up. She made Amina walk back with him to his home. And so the two girls left the stream without seeing the strange red light start to glow in its murky waters.

Martin lived in the Burlington Hotel on the promenade. It was only a small hotel but the girls thought he was dead lucky. His Mum ran the hotel. Mrs Rowlands took one look at Martin and knew he was having one of his asthma attacks.

"It's the traffic," she told her friend Sarah Brightly.

"You could write about traffic fumes."

Sarah was a journalist for the local paper, the *Southbeach Gazette*. Jenny couldn't believe her luck. Secretly, she wanted to be a reporter when she grew up and this was her chance to speak to a real journalist! But Martin made it clear that he didn't want the girls to stay.

There weren't many people staying at the hotel. Business was bad and it wasn't helped by a new mystery illness that had turned up in Southbeach. No-one knew what it was but lots of people had it, particularly children. Even Miss Grant wondered whether it was safe to stay and she was one of the few guests left at the Burlington Hotel. And if she went, her friend Mrs MacDonald would probably go too.

Martin didn't know how bad things were. He liked to shut himself up in his room and look at the sky through his telescope. Nothing seemed very important when you realised how big the Universe was. He was star-gazing that evening when the Chef brought him some dinner. Chef was a good friend really but he was always playing tricks on Martin.

So when Martin suddenly got excited and said he could see a spaceship, Chef thought he was just getting his own back. "You were having me on," he said. "There's nothing there!"

But Martin *had* seen something. Still both Chef and his Mum thought he was making it up. He got very angry and wished it was men from Mars.
"It'll show you!" he shouted.

A bit later, when Miss Grant and Mrs MacDonald were having their dinner, everyone saw the spaceship. Only they didn't know what it was. There were dazzling lights over the sea and then it disappeared. It was all over very quickly, and only Martin realised that it must be the ship he'd seen through his telescope.

Everyone rushed out of the hotel. The street was full of people gazing at the sea. It seemed as if everyone Martin knew was there. Sarah Brightly was on the spot with her notebook. Jenny and Amina were on their way home from the cinema. Then suddenly Martin noticed Mr Belcher. It wasn't the spaceship that had brought him to the promenade though. Mr Belcher was looking for Mrs Rowlands.

Martin was uneasy. He knew that Belcher had been pestering his mother to sell the hotel. Jenny knew who Mr Belcher was too. Her Dad worked for him in his chemicals factory near the beach. Amina didn't trust him; she thought the tide might be bringing pollution up into the stream from the sea near Belcher's factory.

A policeman came along and tried to send everyone away. "There's nothing to worry about," he said. "It was a sudden electrical storm. You can all go home."

Martin and the two girls were the last to leave. The girls thought Martin knew something about the "storm". But they all gave up and went away in the end.

And so no-one saw what walked out of the sea. And even if they had, they wouldn't have known what on earth it was.

2 An uninvited guest

Martin woke up in a cold sweat. All night long men from Mars had been coming to get Mum and Chef. And it was all his fault! It was a relief to wake up on an ordinary Southbeach morning. But was it ordinary? There had been something about last night that needed investigating. Martin decided to go down to the beach.

He wasn't the only one out early. Jenny and Amina were running along the promenade. They spotted Martin on the beach. He was looking down at the sand as if he was following a trail. They decided to spy on him. It was easy at first and they got well ahead of him, but he suddenly changed direction and they had to hide.

That was when they got the shock of their lives! Jenny's scream brought Martin running and they all three stared at what they had found. It was obviously not from earth. It had big scales and was sort of brownish; round but roughly human-shaped. It had a special kind of computer on its wrist, like a big watch. The creature fiddled with it. Then he turned to the children and greeted them in Chinese.

It took a while for the alien to realise that their language was English and when he did he spoke it in a strange way. He told them his name was Ollie and he was from the planet Gia.

"Where's that?" asked Jenny.

"It's a million billion trillion zillion light years and five metres away," said the alien.

They didn't know if he was joking or not. He seemed

terribly hungry and ate Amina's sweets, wrapper and all. But when the children saw the two women from the hotel walking past, Ollie did something even more amazing. He disappeared! He came back when the women had gone and showed the children that he could shrink too.

If only Mrs Rowlands' new guest could have seen that! Joe Lowin had just checked into the Burlington Hotel. He was a journalist on a big national newspaper and he was feeling cross that they had sent him down to a little place like Southbeach. Mystery illnesses and electrical storms were small time stuff for an ace reporter like Joe Lowin. He thought the *Daily News* was making fun of him. They thought he was finished as a top journalist. What he needed was a really big story – a scoop.

And if he had known it, the biggest story in the world was about to happen right here in Southbeach. Ollie was telling the children he needed their help. He wouldn't say why, but the computer on his wrist was showing a kind of countdown. And that meant trouble, big trouble. Only how big they didn't yet understand.

3 Whoops!

The children were beginning to realise just how difficult it was to help an alien. Ollie explained that he had come to Earth to check on a space probe that had been sent out from Gia a hundred years ago.

"We were monitoring pollution across the Universe," he explained. "But suddenly the probe we put here, on Earth, began to overload."

He told them that the pollution levels in Southbeach had become so high that the probe was in danger of exploding – and taking the whole of Southbeach with it! They had just five days to find it and for Ollie to fix it. But there were other problems too. The longer Ollie stayed on Earth, the weaker and clumsier he would get. It had something to do with the atmosphere being different from Gia's. They had to find the probe as quickly as possible.

But meanwhile they had to keep Ollie hidden and safe. They soon decided that the hotel would be the safest place. It was only just across the promenade and Martin could hide Ollie in his room. Getting him there was not so easy. The alien disappeared when he was asked to but in the hotel lobby he managed to knock over Mrs Rowlands' favourite plant stand. The worse thing was that she saw it happen. It looked as if it just toppled over and smashed all by itself!

Then to make matters worse, Ollie decided to mend it with his magic sphere. By the time Mrs Rowlands came back, the plant stand was perfect again. And while she was still staring at it, Ollie realised that he had done the wrong thing. So, to be helpful, he smashed it again!

After so much hard work, he was hungrier than ever. Martin installed Ollie and the girls in his room and went off to the kitchen in search of food. While he was away, Ollie produced

a pollution map of Southbeach on Martin's computer screen, using the machine on his wrist. There were lots of red patches, particularly along the beach. They couldn't believe how bad it was.

But if they could have seen what Mr Belcher was up to in his factory, perhaps they would not have been so surprised. He was emptying chemical waste into the sea while no-one was looking. Only he got someone else to do his dirty work.

The probe began to travel downstream towards the sea, where all the pollution was coming from.

Back at the hotel, Ollie was as clumsy as ever and only slightly less hungry after all the food Martin brought. He was tired of having to disappear, so Jenny came up with the idea of dressing him in some of Martin's clothes. Martin was not pleased with the result. Ollie looked really ridiculous. They all set off in the direction of the factory.

Deep under the water off the shore near the factory, the space probe monitored the pollution which began to flow from Belcher's tanks of chemicals.

4 Code name Charley

Ollie and the three children were on the beach, looking for the space probe. He knew it was somewhere near water. The problem was, the children had no idea what they were looking for.

"Why can't you find this thing yourself?" asked Amina. "Why do you need us?"

The alien looked embarrassed. He had to admit that the instrument for finding the probe had "got clumsied". To take their minds off who had done it, he held out the magic sphere.

Miraculously, four ice-creams appeared! Ollie finished his first. The children were impressed but Ollie admitted he could perform that miracle only once a year. He told them that the probe had a code name. It was called Charley.

"What does that stand for?" asked Jenny.
"Inter-Galactic Pollution Monitoring Device," said Ollie.
"That doesn't spell Charley," protested Martin.

But Ollie said it did where he came from. The children were glad they didn't have to learn Gian. By now they were nearly at the chemicals factory. They didn't see Belcher, sitting in his posh car with his daughter Claire. Ollie was too busy looking at all the ugly litter and rubbish on the beach.

"Grown-ups!" he said disgustedly. The children were amazed. They had just assumed Ollie was a grown-up, but he turned out to be a child too, in Gian years. When they reached the factory, Amina noticed the water near it was even more cloudy than usual. But someone else had noticed them. Mr Belcher came and told them all to clear off. He gave Ollie a suspicious look.

That was the end of probe hunting for the day. Besides Amina thought it was even more urgent to phone the Water Board. She thought they should try to find out if the tide was washing chemicals from the factory upstream. They said they'd send an Inspector to check it out. But while Amina was making her call from the hotel and Jenny was trying to make friends with Sarah Brightly, who had seen Mr Belcher's suspicious behaviour, no-one was keeping an eye on Ollie.

The delicious smell of cake drew him to the kitchen. It was only a moment before he had shrunk so small that Chef couldn't see him. He had soon scoffed almost all of the cake.

By then the children had found out he was missing, not just invisible. They arrived in the kitchen to see one of the last pieces of cake floating in the air. Amina had to pretend she was levitating it by a magic trick. Little did she know how much trouble that would cause later!

They still hadn't found Ollie but they found Mr Belcher in the lobby. One look at him told Amina that he knew about her phone call and that the Water Inspector would find nothing. Mr Belcher had not come looking for her though. He wanted to have another go at persuading Martin's Mum to sell the hotel.

Ollie hadn't finished causing chaos. He knocked over another vase and this time Miss Grant saw it. The sight of a vase toppling over all by itself made her scream and Mrs Rowlands, Belcher, Chef and Joe Lowin, ace reporter, all came running. The children watched helplessly as the door to Martin's room opened all by itself. All the grown-ups walked slowly towards the door. Was Ollie about to be discovered?

5 Mystifying magic

Mrs MacDonald took some time to bring round her friend Miss Grant, who had fainted when she saw the vase smash by itself. If only Ollie could have left well alone! He hadn't learned anything from his earlier adventure with Mrs Rowlands and the plant stand. Miss Grant had just come round, when . . .

"Look!" she screamed.

Mrs MacDonald looked. The vase was putting itself back together.

The other grown-ups, who had all gone into Martin's room, hadn't found anything so amazing. They came running out, just in time to see Miss Grant faint again. The children knew they would have to come up with some sort of explanation. Jenny suddenly remembered Amina's performance in the kitchen.

"Amina does magic tricks," she told Joe Lowin.

The other two caught on really quickly.

"Yes," said Amina, "remember the cake, Chef?"

"Show us another magic trick," said Belcher, as they all went downstairs. He wasn't convinced.

Amina began to panic but it seemed that Ollie had picked up the idea too. The telephone on the reception desk lifted off its hook. Everyone saw. The children sighed with relief. They were off the hook too.

But not for long! Joe Lowin saw his chance of a big story and he was on the other phone before the reception one stopped levitating.

"The greatest magician in the world . . . only twelve . . . It has to go on the front page!"

And that's where it was next day. INCREDIBLE MYSTIFYING MAGIC said the headline. It gave Jenny an idea; she decided to keep a notebook of all that had happened since they met Ollie. It would be good practice for being a journalist when she grew up.

They tried searching the beach again. Amina was still cross with Ollie for doing the mending trick and leaving them to cover up for him. They ended up near the factory again and saw Claire Belcher sitting in her father's car. She seemed to be watching them. They thought she looked really sad.

"I don't think *I'd* be happy with that father," said Amina.

She would have been even more unhappy if she could have seen inside the factory, where Belcher was ordering Jenny's Dad to dump some more waste. Mr Steel refused. He walked out for some fresh air and saw his daughter and her friends on the beach. He knew Amina very well and he recognised Martin but who was that strange-looking child with them? But Mr Steel soon forgot about Ollie. He was too worried about his daughter being near the factory.

"I don't like you near the water," he said.

Back at the hotel, Mrs Rowlands was feeling more worried than ever. Joe Lowin was leaving next day and she had no new guests. She decided to have a talk to Martin about it. He realised for the first time how short of money they were. And he realised that his Mum was going to sell the hotel to Belcher if they didn't get some very soon.

Martin couldn't sleep that night. He even asked Ollie if he could come up with some money but he couldn't. Eventually Martin fell asleep and then it was Ollie's turn to be restless. Even in his sleep he could smell cake. He set off for the kitchen, sleepwalking.

Unfortunately Miss Grant was just coming out of her room as
Ollie sleepwalked down the corridor . . .

6 Monster mayhem

Miss Grant wasn't the only one to get a shock. Mrs MacDonald and Joe Lowin both rushed out of their rooms when they heard the familiar sound of her screaming. And they saw Ollie too. Worst of all, Ollie woke up and saw them. He disappeared.

Joe Lowin went mad with excitement.

"A monster!" he shouted. "An alien! A mutant martial arts wotsit space monster alien ET creature from another planet!"

No wonder Mrs Rowlands and Chef came to see what all the fuss was! Ace reporter Lowin had his big story at last. He was soon gabbling it over the phone to the *Daily News*.

Which was where Jenny and Amina read it next morning. They went straight to the hotel, where they saw a police car. They also saw Sarah Brightly.

"Joe Lowin gets all the good stories," she sighed.

And Joe Lowin was making sure that no-one else was going to get this one. He tried to get Mrs Rowlands to keep everyone out of the hotel. Even Jenny and Amina had to stay outside. Martin and Ollie were keen to get out before Lowin found them. They had to take the fire escape. They met their friends at the bottom.

They were soon back on the beach out of sight of the hotel, but Ollie seemed to be getting worse. He was clumsier than ever. They reached the beach near Belcher's factory just as a new lot of waste was pumped into the water. And Belcher had just told Jenny's Dad he wasn't going to do that any more!

This time Amina had a bottle with her to collect a sample of the polluted water.

"It looks disgusting, doesn't it?" she said.

Then they noticed Claire Belcher watching them from her father's car. Ollie wasn't well and Martin wondered how he could get back to his spaceship, even if they did find Charley in time. But Ollie said the spaceship would come out of the sea if he whistled for it. Ollie felt bad but soon Amina felt worse. She suddenly fainted. Claire came over to help and Belcher and Mr Steel both came out of the factory. Mr Steel picked Amina up and carried her to his car. Mr Belcher was furious.

"You're fired!" he yelled.

"No," said Mr Steel, "I quit."

He drove off with the children but there was no sign of Ollie. Claire picked up the bottle of water that Amina had dropped. She took the top off and sniffed it. Her father was furious with her for getting out of the car.

"Never go on that beach," he said.

But as they drove away, Claire started to feel ill in the same way as Amina. Mr Belcher's anger turned to horror as he realised that she had caught the mystery illness.

7 Doctor Miracle

Sarah Brightly went to visit Amina in the Southbeach Hospital and found Jenny already there. Amina had the mystery illness. In another ward, Claire Belcher was feeling as ill as Amina. The nurse told Mr Belcher they had found a strange bottle in Claire's pocket and they were getting it analysed. Claire told the nurse she had found it on the beach.

The hospital was a popular place that morning. A strange visitor arrived on a bike with Martin running along behind. It was Ollie. But soon he managed to get himself dressed up as a doctor. But when a nurse came to ask his opinion, she was not convinced. He wasn't like any other doctor in Southbeach Hospital!

Martin and Ollie hurried off down a corridor. Ollie heard Jenny reading a poem aloud to Amina and joined in. He seemed to be reading her mind. He was so carried away that he ended up in Claire's ward, not Amina's.

Mr Belcher immediately offered him large sums of money to make Claire better. Ollie managed to escape when a nurse came in, but she had bad news for Belcher. The analysis showed that the bottle contained polluted sea-water. The illness would not be a mystery much longer.

But curing it was another matter. "Doctor" Ollie was now in the right room and he could see how ill Amina was. He took out the magic sphere and said that he could only use it once against illness. He held it out and Amina and Claire were both suddenly cured.

"It's a miracle!" said the nurse.

But as soon as Amina was better, she wanted to get on with the search for Charley. They really were going to need a

miracle to stop Southbeach from being blown up. But they had no better luck that day. When Jenny got home she found her father hadn't had any luck finding a new job either. She wrote in her notebook:

"Mystery illness cured. Still no sign of Charley. Not much time left."

> Day 4 –
>
> Mystery illness cured
> Still no sign of Charley.
> Not much time left.

Joe Lowin was another person who was out of luck. He and the police had searched every inch of the hotel and not found a trace of the alien. He was getting desperate. If he didn't get a lead on it soon he was going to lose his story and he would be a laughing-stock. Then he overheard Chef talking to Martin – about a spaceship. What he didn't know was that Chef had whistled it out of the sea by mistake! His whistle was just like Ollie's. Chef and Martin were both denying seeing the spaceship, but that didn't fool a newshound like Joe Lowin. He guessed that Martin or Chef must have the key to the story. And he thought he knew how to turn it.

8 Betrayed!

Next morning Lowin thought he was hot on the trail. He tried Chef first. He took out a lot of five pound notes and tried to get Chef to tell him about the spaceship. But Chef said "I don't know what you mean, sir" and asked him to leave the kitchen. That left Martin.

Martin was in his room, trying to stop Ollie breaking things. The alien was getting more and more clumsy. In the end Martin had to lock him in. He decided to phone the girls. But on his way to the lobby, he saw Mr Belcher going in to his mother's office. Martin knew that could mean only one thing. As if he didn't have enough to worry about!

Martin went out to wait for the girls on the promenade. But Joe Lowin got to him first.
"Seen any more spaceships?" he asked.

Somehow Martin couldn't stop himself. He told Lowin about Belcher wanting to buy the hotel. The newshound saw his chance.

"Maybe we can help each other," he said.

He offered Martin a lot of money to tell him about the spaceship. Thousands of pounds! If only Martin had known what was happening inside the hotel! Mrs Rowlands had been just about to sign Belcher's contract when people started ringing up to book Magic weekends and Space Trek parties. Joe Lowin's stories had done the hotel some good.

But Martin didn't know. He thought that everything was hopeless. Ollie was ill, his mother was going to sell the hotel and anyway Southbeach would be blown up soon if they couldn't find Charley. What did anything matter? He took Joe Lowin up to his room. He let him in. Ollie was asleep on the bed.

Lowin went bananas! This was his story all right. He grabbed the key from Martin and locked Ollie up again. He wasn't going to let him get away this time! He ran for the phone. Martin was very unhappy. Lowin had promised him money to save the hotel but he hadn't given him any and now he had taken the key. Martin knew already that he had done the wrong thing.

But there was worse to come. His mother told him she didn't have to sell after all. And she thought Martin and his friends had deliberately started the magic and alien stories to bring business to the hotel. Martin realised what an awful thing he had done – and all for nothing. He ran upstairs as fast as he could, yelling "Ollie!" at the top of his voice. "Joe Lowin's coming!"

Joe Lowin was indeed coming, very angry with Martin. And at that moment Jenny and Amina got to the hotel too. They heard the noise and ran upstairs followed by Mrs Rowlands. They reached the top in time to see Joe Lowin open the door with Martin's key. They looked at him in horror. Lowin burst into the room – which was empty. He searched hopelessly for the alien. He didn't know what had happened and Mrs Rowlands knew even less. But Jenny and Amina knew exactly what was going on. Martin had betrayed Ollie!

9 Hunt the Alien

Martin felt terrible. He knew what the girls were thinking and Joe Lowin made it worse by insisting that Martin had told him all about the alien.

"You said its name was Ollie and it came from the planet Gia," he said.

Martin decided to deny everything.

"But these are its clothes!" said Lowin picking up a heap from the floor.

"They're Martin's clothes," said Mrs Rowlands. She was grateful to Lowin for bringing so many guests to the hotel but she really thought he was beginning to go mad about this alien business.

Joe was getting suspicious of Martin.

"You set me up. No-one does this to me!"

He left the room, furious with all of them. But he had mentioned something about money. The girls knew what that meant even if Mrs Rowlands didn't. When she had gone the girls turned on Martin. Amina in particular was furious. "How could you? He *trusted* us and you told on him!"

Martin started to get another asthma attack.
"We were going to have to sell the hotel!" he said.
But Amina wasn't convinced by that explanation. She dragged Jenny off to look for Ollie.

As the two girls came out of the hotel, they ran into a policeman. Lowin had phoned him as soon as he had seen Ollie. Now he had to explain that the alien had disappeared again. Then Lowin remembered something. Martin had said two girls had been with him when he found the alien. He got the policeman to follow Jenny and Amina.

But Martin saw them from the hotel entrance and had an idea. Soon afterwards Lowin spotted a figure dressed like Ollie and shaped liked Ollie riding a bike. He made the policeman follow that instead. The chase was on!

The girls realised it must be Martin trying to make up for what he had done. They searched for Ollie and couldn't find him. But suddenly, in the sea they found Charley! It was flashing a red light. There was not much time left.

Time was running out for Martin too. If he kept biking as hard as that, he would soon be really ill. He took a short cut that the police car couldn't manage. It led to Belcher's factory. And that was where Ollie was hiding. The girls had just found him and told him about Charley when Martin arrived, out of breath. Ollie was lying on the floor of the chemicals store. He was too weak to do anything about the probe.

"I'm really sorry," said Martin.

Amina was still cross with Martin but he had the bright idea of using the magic sphere. They all held on to it and wished hard to make Ollie better. They were concentrating so much they didn't hear Mr Belcher's car draw up outside.

10 The final countdown

The magic sphere worked but just as Ollie was getting to his feet, the door to the store slammed shut and there was the sound of a key being turned in the lock. Mr Belcher had trapped them!

But he hadn't realised how Claire would react. His daughter had come with him in the car as usual and when he went back to use his car phone, she realised what was going on.

He was telling the police that he had caught the alien. Claire tried to stop him. He thought if he handed the alien over to the police, he could somehow make it take the blame for all the pollution. But Claire knew better. She broke the phone and ran to the store.

Inside, the children had just realised that there was only ten minutes left before the probe blew up. Claire tried to persuade her father to hand over the key but it took up precious time. By the time she released the others, they could hear a police car on the way. It was the one with Joe Lowin in it. The children hurried Ollie away and Mr Belcher suddenly changed his mind. "This way!" he shouted. But he led Lowin and the policeman in the wrong direction.

But his factory was pumping out more pollution into the water where the probe was. As it reached Charley, there was a violent reaction from the probe. For a moment the children thought they were too late and when Mr Belcher saw what was happening, he realised just how much danger they were all in. Sarah Brightly arrived on her bike in time to see the flashing lights. She had been following the police car.

Ollie stepped into the murky water. The clock on his wrist showed there were only ten seconds left. It was now or never. But the second that Ollie had fixed the probe he was in almost as great danger from Joe Lowin. It was Mr Belcher who stopped him from grabbing Ollie. He hung on tight to him while Ollie said goodbye to his Earth friends. Ollie gave Amina the magic sphere. He hugged them all, even Martin to show he was forgiven. As Ollie walked into the sea whistling for his spaceship, Mr Belcher was arrested.

The hotel was busier than it had ever been. It was full of Space Trekkers. They were all in the dining room when there was a loud noise and a dazzling display of lights over the sea. They all thought Mrs Rowlands had organised it just for them. The Burlington Hotel was definitely a hit!

And so was Jenny. The policeman wanted to interview the children about what had been going on, but Jenny already had it all written down in her journal. She promised to give it to Sarah Brightly when the police had finished with it. Joe Lowin couldn't believe his ears – he had been scooped by the *Southbeach Gazette!*